Jack Kent's TWELVE DAYS of CHRISTMAS

SCHOLASTIC INC. New York Toronto London Auckland Sydney

ISBN 0-590-06163-1

Illustrations copyright © 1973 by Jack Kent. This edition is published by Scholastic Inc., by arrangement with Parents Magazine Press.

16 15 14 13 12 11 10 9 8 7 6   2 3/9

Printed in the U.S.A.   08

On the first day of Christmas
my true love gave to me
a partridge in a pear tree.

On the second day of Christmas
my true love gave to me
two turtledoves and
a partridge in a pear tree.

On the third day of Christmas
my true love gave to me
three French hens, two turtledoves,
and a partridge in a pear tree.

On the fourth day of Christmas my true love gave to me
four collie birds, three French hens, two turtledoves, and a
partridge in a pear tree.

On the fifth day of Christmas my true love
gave to me five golden rings, four collie birds,
three French hens, two turtledoves, and a
partridge in a pear tree.

On the sixth day of Christmas my true love gave to me six geese
a-laying, five golden rings, four collie birds, three French hens,
two turtledoves, and a partridge in a pear tree.

On the seventh day
of Christmas
my true love gave to me
seven swans a-swimming,
six geese a-laying,
five golden rings,
four collie birds,
three French hens,
two turtledoves,
and a partridge
in a pear tree.

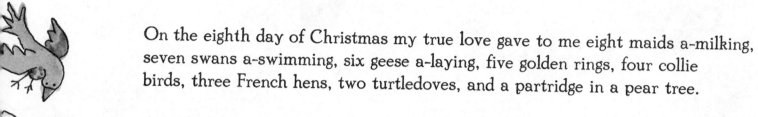

On the eighth day of Christmas my true love gave to me eight maids a-milking, seven swans a-swimming, six geese a-laying, five golden rings, four collie birds, three French hens, two turtledoves, and a partridge in a pear tree.

On the ninth day of Christmas my
true love gave to me nine pipers
piping, eight maids a-milking, seven
swans a-swimming, six geese a-laying,
five golden rings, four collie birds,
three French hens, two turtledoves,
and a partridge in a pear tree.

On the tenth day of Christmas my true love
gave to me ten drummers drumming,
nine pipers piping, eight maids a-milking,
seven swans a-swimming, six geese a-laying,
five golden rings, four collie birds,
three French hens, two turtledoves,
and a partridge in a pear tree.

On the eleventh day of Christmas
my true love gave to me eleven lords
a-leaping, ten drummers drumming,
nine pipers piping, eight maids
a-milking, seven swans a-swimming,
six geese a-laying, five golden rings,
four collie birds, three French hens,
two turtledoves, and a partridge
in a pear tree.

On the twelfth day of Christmas my true love gave to me twelve ladies dancing, eleven lords a-leaping, ten drummers drumming, nine pipers piping,

eight maids a-milking, seven swans a-swimming, six geese a-laying, five golden rings, four collie birds, three French hens, two turtledoves...

... and a partridge in a pear tree.